Devin Staurbringer is a writer living in Ohio. His children's book, *Hope the Hopeful Piglet,* won the 2023 North Coast Indie Author Book Award for reader's favorite author. He hopes to travel the world and write many books. He is passionate about trying to make the world a better place through activism and writing. This is his first novella.

For those who feel lost, may we find our way.

Devin Staurbringer

TIDES OF REVELATION

AUSTIN MACAULEY PUBLISHERS™

LONDON • CAMBRIDGE • NEW YORK • SHARJAH

Ordering Information
Quantity sales: Special discounts are available on quantity purchases by corporations, associations, and others. For details, contact the publisher at the address below.

Publisher's Cataloging-in-Publication data
Staurbringer, Devin
Tides of Revelation

ISBN 9798889107354 (Paperback)
ISBN 9798889107606 (ePub e-book)

Library of Congress Control Number: 2024907155

www.austinmacauley.com/us

First Published 2024
Austin Macauley Publishers LLC
40 Wall Street, 33rd Floor, Suite 3302
New York, NY 10005
USA

mail-usa@austinmacauley.com
+1 (646) 5125767

Thank you to my family and friends for their love and support. And thank you to the team at Austin Macauley.

"Ourself behind ourself, concealed should startle most."
– Emily Dickinson

Day 1
Thursday

Hanna

The tides were the first to stop. It was Thursday, around noon, and I was driving up to the lake house to meet with the others. We hadn't seen each other in years, close to a decade, but recently reconnected on social media and decided to meet up. We all met during our last year in college and then went our separate ways. So we, we being Jane, Pete, Derrick, and myself, rented a lake house on *Airbnb* for five days. I was certain that I was going to be the first one there; I always liked to be early.

The road I was on wound through a beautiful forest. In and out of trees. No other roads or cars in sight. It was late in the summer, and everything was so green, vibrant, almost dripping with color. The sun was at its highest, and the light hit the tops of the trees and then broke apart into smaller beams that fell onto the road in front of me. The drive seemed to go on forever. And I was fine with that. The wind gently blew the leaves of the trees, causing them to flap around in the way that they do. I peered left and right, into the deep brown and green of the woods. I saw deer, so many deer. More than I had seen in a long time. Living in the city, I didn't get out to the woods as often as I'd like.

I turned the music off and the air conditioning too. Then I rolled down all the windows and leaned my head slightly out of the car. The wind immediately loosened my hair from the tight bun I had it in, but I didn't care. I took in all the sounds—the birds, the leaves, the wind. The deer were running through the forest as I drove past. Just then, one of the deer leaped out of the trees on the left side and into the road in front of me. I slammed on the breaks and yanked the wheel to the right. The car swerved into the tree line and came to a stop when it slammed into a tree.

Luckily, I hadn't been going too fast, but nonetheless, the car was not going to be drivable. The hood of the car was wrapped in a 'U' shape around the tree. Smoke started to curl out as I stared at it through the cracked windshield. I was in a daze, and my vision was a bit fuzzy. I looked at myself in the rearview mirror and I had a cut on my forehead. I must have hit my head on the steering wheel. A little blood dripped down off my forehead and onto my lap. I sat for a moment with my head down trying to collect myself.

What the hell do I do now? I thought.

I lifted my head and looked out the driver side window, and there it was—the deer. It was still standing there, right next to the car, its face just a few feet away from mine, staring at me. We looked into each other's eyes for what seemed like an eternity. I almost forgot all about what just happened. For some reason, I reached my hand out toward it. And for some reason, it took a step toward my hand. Its nose wiggled like a cat or dog when they sniff you. Then it blinked, turned around, and ran off back into the woods.

I came back to the reality of my situation. I didn't need an ambulance; I knew that much. And I didn't want to get the cops involved, so I'd have to walk the rest of the way to the beach house. Either that or wait for someone to be driving down the road. But the road only goes to the beach house, so the only people that would be driving on it would be Pete, Jane, or Derrick, and they wouldn't be coming for hours. Damn me and my stupid need to be early.

Looks like I'm walking, I thought.

I grabbed my phone from the dashboard and looked at the GPS that I had been following. It said that I was about a mile away from the beach house. I found my bag on the floor of the passenger side, stuck my phone in one of the pockets, and opened the door. I wasn't going to drag my luggage all the way there. I figured I could just use someone else's car to retrieve my bags later when they showed up. I threw my bag over my shoulder and started hoofing it.

I was still a little woozy as I wobbled my way down the road. I took my shoes off and jammed them in my bag. Walking in my bare feet somehow felt more stable and secure. Not that my shoes were unstable, they weren't high heels or anything, which I never wore; they were just regular sneakers. But somehow the sensation of my feet on the ground made me feel better. And the warm pavement on my skin was nice as well.

The sun shimmered through the branches as the early afternoon began. The road ceased its twisting and turning, and all the bends became straight as I continued my walk. At the end of the long road, I could see the house come into view. I started to feel better just seeing the house. I needed to lie down. Just then, I heard something behind me. I swiveled my head back and there in the road was the deer. It was walking with me—following me. About 100 feet behind. I stopped walking and turned all the way around to face it. And it stopped walking too. I started walking backwards with my eyes locked on it. It began to walk again. I stopped. It stopped. I started. It started. It was a male deer, with a majestic set of antlers. The sun rays hit him and the scene looked like a painting.

I just wanted to get to a bed, so I turned around back toward the house. I could still hear its hooves clacking on the concrete.

Why the hell is this thing following me? I thought.

But I honestly didn't care. I was just so tired. Eventually, the house was so close that I could smell the sea beyond it. The forest fell away, and the surroundings opened up. The house was situated on a big piece of land, a few trees scattered around the grounds but mostly open yard. On the other side of the house was a little drop off with stairs down to the beach and then the endless ocean.

I got to the front door of the house, and the key was under the welcome mat, just like the owner said it would be. When I bent down, however, my head began spinning and I knew I had to sit down. I slid the key into the handle and turned until I heard a click. I opened the door and went in. I threw the key on the table by the door and dropped my bag on the ground. The décor of the house was that of the typical beach house that is rented out. Pictures of the beach in frames with seashells on them. The starfish motif as far as the eye could see. Beach towels and umbrellas stacked in the closet. And don't get me started on the bathroom.

I went into the kitchen and got myself a glass of water. I drank it in one big chug and filled the glass up again. I looked out through the windows in the kitchen. It was such a fantastic view of the beach and ocean. I slid a chair up to the window and sat down to finish the rest of my water. It was only then, after the relief that came with sitting, that I realized I probably shouldn't let myself fall asleep. At least not for a while. Can't be too careful with head injuries. So, I got up and walked over to the sink. I ran the cold water for a moment and then cupped my hands under the faucet. I lowered my head and threw the cold water on my face. It felt so good, and it definitely woke me up a bit. I did it again, and one more time. I dried my face and hands with a towel and checked to see if my cut was still bleeding. It wasn't.

What should I do? I thought to myself. And then I decided to have a walk down to the beach.

The cacophonous sound of seagulls rang in the air as I walked down the boardwalk and on to the beach. I took my shoes and socks off and dug my toes into the sand. It was warm and soft. I couldn't remember the last time I was barefoot on a beach. Must have been when I was little. My parents would bring me to the beach on the weekends sometimes. I never really liked it though. They seemed to really enjoy it, so I kept going and didn't say anything for their sake. It wasn't really that bad of a time. I just didn't like getting wet and sandy.

But now that I'm an adult, standing there on the beach, I get the appeal. It's almost like it's a place disconnected from time and space. It seems to never change. Though I understand that landscape is constantly changing, the beach seems to be frozen in time, unchanging, reliable, always there. A silent mystery.

I walked down to the water's edge where the tide was sliding across the sand. The soft foam waves gently crested on the shore and slowly rolled back into the sea. Then another wave came and went. Then another. Each wave, just one in an endless sequence. Ceaselessly coming and going. In and out. Back and forth. Like the sea is breathing. I wadded into the water until I was standing shin-deep. I looked out at the horizon and for a split-second, I almost didn't believe it was real. If anything was real, how… how could something like this exist?

As I stood in the water, the waves gently washed across my shins. I looked down and watched the white foam roll over my feet. I matched my breathing with the movement of the waves. In and out. In and out. Nothing but the all-consuming sound of the waves and the wind. After some time—I don't know how long—I saw a red drop of blood fall from my forehead and land in the wet sand as the tide was out. And in an instant, the tide came back and the red was washed over and taken away by the waves. The cut on my forehead must have started bleeding again. I looked up and stared out at the horizon, and I could feel another drop of blood roll down my face. I wiped my face with the inside of my sleeve and held it there until it stopped bleeding. Just as I was about to sit down on the shore, I heard a voice call out from behind me.

"Hanna!? Is that you?"

I turned around to see Derrick on the back deck of the house. He was wearing a button-up beach shirt and had a hat on. I looked at him and thought, *Is that really Derrick? He looks so different.*

It had been nearly a decade. People change, unlike the repetitive and reliable waves. He had short black hair and was sharply dressed in slacks and a button-up.

"Hey! Yeah, it's me," I called back. I glanced back at the sea and then turned to walk back to the house. I grabbed my shoes and socks from the edge of the boardwalk and continued up to the back deck of the house. Derrick was standing at the top of the stairs waiting for me with his arms outstretched. We hugged and walked over to the chairs and sat down.

"My gosh! Hanna in the flesh! How the heck have you been?" Derrick said with a smile.

"Well, I've been living. You know how it is," I said, realizing that I was completely unprepared for all the catch-up small talk that was going to happen.

"That's great! The last time we talked, before we all went our own ways, you were wanting to work in a library if I recall correctly. Did you every end up doing that?" "Oh yeah, I did it, and I'm still doing it."

"How's that going?"

"Good, it's a better job than most, I guess. What about you? What have you been up to?"

"Well, I've just been living my dream. I'm a freelance photojournalist. I travel all over the place, take pictures, and report on things going on in the world."

"That sounds really interesting. You'll have to show me some of your work this week."

"Most definitely, I would love… uhm Hanna, I think you've got a cut on your forehead that's bleeding."

"Oh yeah," I said as I wiped the blood with my sleeve again. "I had a little accident on my drive up."

"Was that your car on the side of the road I saw coming in? Are you okay?"

"Yeah, it was my car. And yeah, I'm okay. It's just a small cut."

"Okay, good. I'm glad you're safe and relatively unharmed. I was wondering why I didn't see your car in the driveway when I got here. What happened?"

"Well, there were these deer running in the woods next to my car. And then one of them jumped into the road and I swerved and hit a tree. Speaking of that, would you mind driving me back to my car so I can get the rest of my stuff?"

"Sorry, I don't have a car here. I flew in and took a taxi from the airport. But I'm sure Jane or Pete would be happy to give you a ride, if either of them drives up. Speaking of deer, there was one standing in the front yard when I pulled up."

"Oh, he's still there?"

"You mean he was there when you got here too?"

"Sort of. He actually followed me here on the walk from my car. That's the deer that I swerved to avoid hitting."

"That's strange. He just followed you here and is hanging around out front."

"Yeah, I guess he's my new friend. Well, do you want to head inside and get settled while we wait for the others?"

We stood up and he walked ahead of me into the house through the sliding glass door. Derrick walked through the kitchen and into the living room. He grabbed his bag and headed up stairs to find a bedroom. I walked over to the kitchen sink and grabbed a paper towel. I pressed it against my forehead, wishing the damn cut would stop bleeding. The smart idea finally popped into my head to check for bandages in the bathroom. I walked down the hall and into the tiny bathroom, the upside-down seashell-shaped sink was directly in front of the toilet. You could literally wash your hands while sitting on the crapper.

The medicine cabinet above the sink was framed in brown wood with little white seashells lining the edges. I grabbed the handle and popped it open. It was completely empty. The owner must have cleaned it out before we got here. Nonetheless, I thought I should at least check the upstairs bathroom as well. So, I walked out across the living room and headed up the stairs. The wood under my feet creaked loudly.

"Hanna?" Derrick called from upstairs.

"Yeah, just me. I'm coming to check the bathroom for some bandages for my forehead."

"Good idea."

"Did you find a room you like?"

"Yeah, I got the one over here." He stepped out of his room as I reached the top of the stairs. He had picked the room that was on the left, on the front side of the house. I hadn't picked a room yet, but I thought the back side of the house would be nice, there being a view of the ocean and all.

"I guess I'll take the one opposite you," I said as I pointed toward the room.

"Sounds good," he said.

I walked into the bathroom, which was much bigger than the downstairs one. This bathroom had a huge claw-foot bathtub and a skylight in the roof. The room was bright and spacious. Fresh towels on a table next to the bathtub, of course covered in seashells. I looked over to the wall above the sink and there was a matching medicine cabinet to the one downstairs.

As I walked over, I thought, *Please have some fucking bandages.* I opened it. *Score!*

A half empty box of bandages, along with an empty toothbrush cup, an unopened packet of tissues, and a container of cotton ear swabs.

I took one of the bandages out of the box, peeled the white plastic off the back, looked in the mirror, and put the brown bandage over my cut.

There, that takes care of that, I thought as I crumpled up the wrapper and threw it into the beach-themed garbage can next to the sink. Took a look at myself in the mirror, tightened the loose bun in my hair, turned around, and walked out. I strolled past all the bedrooms, taking a peek in each of them. I got to Derrick's room and stood in the doorway. He was taking clothes out of his suitcase and placing them on the shelf.

"Getting settled in okay?" I said.

"Oh yeah, this is such a nice little place," he said as he looked up at me. Then added, "Hey, looks like there were bandages in the bathroom." He pointed at my head.

"Yep, I'm glad I found some. That cut was getting annoying." I walked into his room and across to the other side by the window. I stood there looking out on the front yard and the driveway. The handful of trees scattered across the big open grounds. My eyes scanned around at all the greenery and finally landed on a big tree. And there, standing under the tree, was that damn deer, just calmly looking around as if it didn't have anywhere else to be. I shook my head and turned around. And up in the corner of the room, I saw a little spider in a web.

"Heads up, there's a spider in the corner," I said as I pointed to the corner of the ceiling.

"Oh, I'm sure he's fine," Derrick said as he looked up at the spider. "I'll leave him alone. We're all God's creatures after all."

I smiled and walked over to my room to check it out more closely. It was similar to Derrick's. Generic full bed, with sand-colored bedding, framed pictures of beaches on the wall, and a cream-colored dresser. I walked over to the window and looked out on the majestic view of the beach and the endless ocean. I fell into a deep thought again.

It's so immense. The ocean is really one of the only places on Earth where we feel our insignificance. Your tininess. Other geographical features such as mountains and canyons have a similar effect. But the ocean is so unfathomably big. And in our day-to-day life, we don't really see the true scale of things. We drive our little car up and down the same small streets. We park in tiny spots. Walk into the little buildings. Sit at the small desks. Write with the tiny pens. Scroll through the little phones. And eat the small food. All the while, the ocean looms in its enormity. It could swallow us, in all our triviality without hesitation. Like a pebble dropped into the middle of the sea, gulped down completely unnoticed. And Earth too, the Earth is like a pebble in the vast ocean of space. I began to feel my pulse quicken and my head felt dizzy. I had to stop thinking; I always get existential panic attacks when I think about our size in all the endlessness.

I took a step back away from the window and took a few deep breaths. I sat on the edge of the bed and took out my phone as a distraction. I needed to pull myself back into the insignificant, the mundanity of everyday life. Just then, my phone vibrated in my hand, it was a text from Jane.

It said, *"We're here."*

We're here, I thought. *Who's we?*

I called out to Derrick, "Jane's here." I stood up and walked back into Derrick's room. He was still unpacking, and I walked past him and over to the window.

"That's great!" he said without looking up from what he was doing. From the window, I saw a car coming up the driveway. It parked, and two people got out of the back. It was Jane and Pete. Why had they come together? And who was driving?

"Oh, it's Jane and Pete," I said to Derrick.

"They're both here? Wonderful!"

"Let's go down and welcome them," I said, and I walked over to the stairs and walked down, the old wood creaking with every step. I walked to the front door, opened it, and stepped out onto the front porch. Jane and Pete were walking up the sidewalk, both dragging luggage behind them. The car they got out of was driving down the driveway, disappearing down the winding road back into the forest. I caught a glimpse of my deer buddy across the yard by the tree line, still just standing there.

"Look who it is!" I called out from the porch.

"Hey there!" Jane said with a smile.

"Hanna banana!" Pete said. "I had completely forgotten that's what he used to call me."

"I completely forgot that's what you used to call me."

"How could you forget the banana?" Pete said. The two of them stepped up the few stairs and walked onto the porch. I hugged each of them, turned around, and open the door into the house. I held it open while the rolled their bags into the living room. Jane looked fantastic, way better than I remembered her. Her hair, once brown, was now an almost white blond. Her face was sharp but warm and welcoming. Pete looked the same as I remembered him. He hadn't changed a bit—short brown hair, defined facial features, and solid body build.

"This place is great!" Jane said, looking around.

"Yeah, it's really relaxing," I said. "Derrick is upstairs unpacking. Why don't you two head up and drop your bags off in your rooms? Mine's the one across from Derrick's."

The two of them headed up the stairs and I walked through the kitchen and back out onto the back balcony. I could hear the stairs creak from all the way outside. I could also hear the faint sound of pleasantries being shared between the three of them. I sat down in a chair and turned my gaze back to the sea. The sun was getting lower. It was a few hours away from touching the horizon where the water meets the sky in a defined, straight line. Below the line, the waves, ceaselessly undulating, bobbing up and down. Above the line, the sky, locked in a solid, stationary state. The clouds and sun move across the sky, but the sky itself is fixed in its position. Two worlds, the moving and the unmoving, the chaotic and the tranquil, the perpetual and the permanent.

"Hanna! Where are you?" Pete called from upstairs. His voice pulled me back into the present moment.

"I'm out back!" I called out. Moments later, I heard the three of them coming down the stairs. They walked through the kitchen and came out to the balcony.

"We're all hungry. What about you?" Derrick said.

"Yeah, I could eat," I said.

"What should we do for dinner?" Jane asked.

"Don't worry about that; I brought a lot of good food. I'll get started on it," Pete said as he walked back into the kitchen and started rummaging around. Derrick and Jane sat down with me on the balcony.

"My gosh! Look at that view," Jane said.

"Isn't it fantastic?" Derrick replied.

"So, Jane, why did you and Pete come together in the same car?" I asked.

"Well, as you know, we actually live kind of close to each other. He and I reconnected maybe a year ago because we ran into each other at a kid's play space, daycare-type place. I was picking up my daughters and he was picking up his son. So he and I had been getting caught up for a while. And we decided to fly in together and share an *Uber* instead of flying separate or driving all the way here."

"That makes sense. So tell me about your daughters, and how's the hubby?" I said.

"Well, Aubrey and Audrey are my little angels, well one's an angel, the other is a bit of a demon child sometimes. And Nathan is doing great, super busy at work. Things are great. How are you doing?"

"I'm well, still living in the area, about a three-hour drive from here. Never got out into the world like you three did."

"So you did drive here? Where's your car? Was that it on the side of the road on the drive in?" she said with a genuine look of concern on her face.

"Yeah, I had a bit of an accident. A deer jumped into the road, and I swerved and hit the tree. I was hoping that you or Pete could give me a ride back to my car so I could get the rest of my bags. But I guess it looks like I'll be hoofing it. But it's a nice walk. I'll do it after diner."

"And you have a boyfriend, correct?"

"Yeah, Jack."

"How's that going? It must be getting serious. You've been together so long."

"I don't know; I'm kind of on the fence as of right now. You know what I mean?"

"Sure, I totally get it. You've got to do what your heart feels is best."

I didn't want to talk about how Jack was an ass, and how he was a bit of a narcissist and emotional manipulator. Jane seemed so together and happy, talking about my problems would feel pathetic.

Turning to Derrick, Jane said, "And you are a traveling freelance journalist? That's fantastic? Are you seeing anyone?"

"No, no, the travel life doesn't afford much time to get to know people," he replied.

The three of us sat back in our seats and looked out to the sea, Pete still making a commotion in the kitchen. The wind blew and the waves rolled across the shore. The view from the balcony really looked like one the photographs or paintings hanging on the walls in the house. It was perfect—the sun, the blue sky, the white clouds, the endless water, the golden sand. What magic happened to create this setting? The matter that makes me, and the matter that makes the sand, the sea, and the sky, all that matter, was once in the same place, somewhere far across the blackness of space. The water, the sand, and me. We were made billions of years ago. Set on a course for this moment now. Destined to meet again.

"I'm going to take a walk down the beach," Jane said as she stood up.

"Okay, we'll give a shout if dinner is ready before you're back," Derrick said.

I was still vaguely hypnotized by the water, but I still heard what Jane and Derrick had said, so I put on a smile and nodded. Jane walked down the back stairs and across the boardwalk and onto the beach. She looked so beautiful walking through that scenery, almost like she belonged to the landscape and was a part of it. Her sandy blond hair matched the sand on the beach.

A few minutes later, I got up and walked into the kitchen. I figured I should get the small talk with Pete out of the way. I walked in through the door and pulled out a seat at the dinner table. Pete saw me walk in but didn't look up from his pots and pans.

"Hey there, Hanna banana."

"Hey, so Pete, how goes it?" I said.

"Pretty damn good. How about you?"

"Oh, you know, things are good. So, you have a son? How's he doing? How's the wife?"

"Little Luke is doing great, super smart. And Elisa is wonderful. She just got a promotion. Everything is really great."

"That's wonderful. Jane was talking about you two ended up moving to the same area and you ran into each other at a kid play place? What are the odds of that?"

"Yeah, it was great to have a friend in the area, especially for our kids. They have someone to go on play dates with. So, was that your car on the side of the road on the way in here?"

"Unfortunately, yes. I had a bit of an accident. A deer jumped into the road, and I swerved into a tree. And yes, before you ask, it is the deer standing in the front yard. And no, I have no idea why he followed me here."

"That's pretty weird. But you're okay, right?"

"Yeah, just a little cut on my forehead."

"That's good."

"After dinner, I think I might walk back to my car and grab the rest of my bags. I was hoping one of you would have a car to give me a ride. But it looks like I'm walking. Oh well, it's not too bad of a walk anyway."

"Well, dinner will be ready in ten or so."

"I'll go tell Derrick and Jane."

I got up and walked out the back door. Derrick was still sitting there looking at the water. Jane was a little way down the beach. I shouted her name, but she couldn't hear me over the sound of the waves and wind. So, I set off down the boardwalk and onto the beach. I loved the feel of the sand between my toes. For some reason, I started walking faster, then moved into a jog, and then broke out into a full sprint. If felt good. It felt like when I used to run on the beaches and through the forests as a child. It was complete freedom, all my thoughts and problems falling behind me. It was so nice that I almost ran right past Jane. But I stopped running when I got close to her, and I walked up next to her.

"Hey, dinner's ready soon," I said, a little out of breath.

"Oh, thanks. I'll be there in a few minutes," Jane said softly. I noticed that it looked like she had been crying—watery, red eyes and a little sniffle.

"Are you okay?"

"Yeah, fine, why?"

"Just wondering. Okay... uhm... I'm going to head back. See you in a bit."

"Okay, sounds good. I'll be along in a minute."

I turned around and walked back to the house. I didn't tell Derrick about Jane possibly crying. I just sat down in one of the deck chairs. I could see Jane walking towards us. She climbed the stairs just as Pete brought the food out onto the balcony.

"We're eating out here?" Derrick said.

"Yeah, why not?" Pete said as he put the plates down on the table.

"I think it'd be nice to eat out here," Jane said, grabbing a chair and sitting down.

"Fine by me," I said.

"That decides it, I guess," Derrick said.

We ate and talked and talked and ate. Pete told us about his wife's promotion and how well his son was doing in school. Jane talked about how her daughters and Pete's son got along so well. Derrick regaled us with tales of his travels. And I, well, I told them the mundane story of me. Same job, same city, same boyfriend. They all feigned enthusiasm and pretended to be intrigued. But I could see it on their faces. They felt bad. How pathetic I was!

We sat in a silence, just finishing up the meal and looking out at the water. We pushed our plates away and leaned back when suddenly, for no reason, I blurted out, "I think I might break up with Jack." No one said anything for a moment.

"Really?" Jane asked and continued, "Why's that?"

"He's, well… he's, sometimes, not all the time, but sometimes he can get angry," I said.

"Angry how?" Derrick asked, leaning forward in his chair.

"Does he hit you?" Pete asked.

"No. Well, sometimes… no. No. He just has a violent temper," I said.

"Still, that's not okay. If he's making you uncomfortable, maybe you should leave him. Have you two talked about it? Does he understand what he's doing?" Jane said.

"Yeah, we've talked about it. And he always says that he'll work on it. He even said he'd go to therapy, but the years pass by, and he's never gone, and he's never changed. But to be honest, I haven't changed either. I have shit that I need to work on too."

"We all do, but that's not an excuse to be abusive to someone," Derrick said.

"Maybe breaking up with him is what you should do," Pete said.

"Yeah, maybe. I just don't know. I think I'm going to take a walk back to my car and get the rest of my stuff. Then we'll head down to the water and watch the sunset." I stood up, grabbed my plate, and walked back into the kitchen. I put my plate in the sink and called out to the others, "I'll be right back."

"Okay, sounds good. See you in a bit," Jane said.

I walked through the house, grabbed my keys off the table, and headed out the front door. I walked down the winding sidewalk to the driveway and out onto the road. I was so distracted by thinking about Jack that I didn't even notice the deer started walking behind me. Once I was further out on the road, I heard the sound of hooves on the pavement. I turned around, and sure enough, there he was. I just kept walking. I was so angry at Jack, at what he did to me, at myself for staying with him for so long, and at myself for not standing up for myself.

I have to leave him. I thought. *I can't let him hurt me anymore.*

I didn't want to tell the others that he did hit me sometimes. I'm sure they assumed as much anyway. I just couldn't say it out loud. And maybe I deserved it. Maybe I was bringing it on myself.

I tried to forget about Jack, so I started looking around at the trees. How wonderful they were! Like another world. I thought that I should get out of the city. Maybe move out here. Or somewhere with lots of trees. Or water. Or mountains. Maybe I'll figure my life out.

Why not? I thought. *Why not?*

I eventually reached my car, and I looked back over my shoulder at the deer who was standing in the road about 50 yards back.

"You did this," I said to him. I unlocked the door and sat in the driver seat. I put the key into the ignition and turned it. Nothing happened. I removed the key and popped the trunk. I grabbed my backpack and slung it over my shoulders. And I pulled my rolling luggage out, put it on the ground, and extended the handle. I closed the trunk and started walking back to the house.

The deer saw me coming and he turned around and headed down the road toward the house as well. As I walked along, dragging my suitcase, I thought about the fact that there have been so many times in my life when if I just made one little change, everything would change. I thought about how life is full of tiny moments, that if handled even minutely differently, everything would be different. I thought about how not making decisions is still a kind of decision-making. Not changing is choosing not to change.

Before I realized, I was back at the house. The deer back at his tree. I walked in, dropped my bags in the living room, and headed back out to the balcony. Pete, Jane, and Derrick were talking when I opened the door and stepped out. They all looked up at me simultaneously.

"Hanna banana! Just in time for the sunset," Pete said.

"How was the walk? Were you able to get all your bags?" Jane asked.

"It was a nice walk. And yeah, I got all my stuff," I said.

"Good, I'm glad," she replied.

"So, are we ready to head down to the beach and watch the sunset?" I asked.

"Let's go!" Pete said.

We all walked down the stairs and across the board walk. I took my shoes off and left them on the stairs. We headed right up to the shoreline. The waves crashed and retreated. They made such a loud sound that even the seagulls squawks were drowned out. The sun was starting to merge with the horizon. The colors in the sky were layered, but the layers were blending into each other.

Orange into red into pink into purple into blue. I waded into the water and tides came in, and then went out. In and then out. And in, and then out. And then… they stopped. The tides stopped. The water just bobbed up and down.

The sea sat as still as a puddle in a parking lot, as calm as a glass of water. Not a single ripple or undulation. Not a wave. Not a sound. The sea was silent. I walked around in the water, splashing with my feet. The water moved when I kicked it, but the tides were no longer sliding up and down the shore. Not a sound except for the wind, and the gulls.

"What the hell?" Pete asked.

"Did the water just stop moving?" Jane added.

"That's really weird, right?" Derrick said.

"Yeah, this is strange," I said as I walked out of the water and back onto the shore.

"I've literally never seen that before. What do you think caused it?" Jane asked.

"I don't know. It's supposed to be a full moon tonight. Maybe that has something to do with it. Or maybe it means a storm is coming. Really, your guess is as good as mine," Pete said.

"Maybe it's some rare phenomenon or something," Derrick said.

"Either way, it looks pretty cool," I said. "And it's so quiet now."

We stood there, not talking, for a few minutes, just existing in the strange silence. The sun dropped lower and lower. It got darker and darker. Behind us, a full moon was rising. It was so big and bright. The silver-white light illuminated the motionless sea.

"Well, I saw a fire pit on the side of the house. Shall we have a fire and crack open a bottle of wine or two?" Pete said.

"Sure, why not?" Jane said.

We all walked back across the sand and up onto the boardwalk. Derrick, Jane, and I headed to the side of the house to where the fire pit was. Pete headed into the house to grab the wine. The fire pit was square and made of stone. It sat on a slab of concrete with eight chairs placed around it. The fire pit was gas-powered with some knobs on the side.

"How do we start this thing?" Derrick asked.

"We have one similar to this at our house. Let me see if I can get it going," Jane said as she started to fiddle with the controls. In a few seconds, she had the flames going. And shortly thereafter, Pete came out with four glasses and two bottles.

"Party time!" Pete exclaimed as he handed out the glasses to us and took a seat. The four of us sat on each side of the square fire pit. Pete opened the first bottle and poured himself a glass before handing the bottle to me. I poured my glass and handed the bottle to Jane, who poured her glass and tried to hand it to Derrick who was on his phone.

"Hey, Derrick, wine," Jane said.

"Sorry, I'm looking up 'ocean tides stopping' and I can't find anything. All I keep reading is that if the tides are moving out away from the shore, and they keep going further and further, and not coming back, that means we need to run and get to high ground because a tsunami is coming," Derrick said.

"Yeah, I remember learning that when I was a kid," Jane said.

"Same here. But that's not what the tides are doing. They're just sitting there," I said.

"And if a tsunami is coming, we are screwed. So, let's drink!" Pete said as he raised his glass. Derrick slid his phone back in his pocket and poured his glass of wine. We all raised our glasses and Pete said, "To old friends and good times."

"Cheers," we all said simultaneously.

As it got darker and darker, more and more lightning bugs began to flicker their lights all around us. The yard and the forest were full of their little yellow illuminations. Like embers from a fire being blown on the breeze. Or a million stars scattered across the darkness of space. We drank and reminisced and drank and laughed. Pete was drinking faster than the rest of us, and he opened the second bottle of wine without saying anything. He poured himself a glass and drank it, almost chugging it, and quickly poured another.

"I miss you guys!" Pete said loudly.

"We miss you too," I said.

"Hanna banana! You're the best! I've always liked you. You know, I had big crush on you in college," he said.

We all sat in the awkward silence for a moment. Then I said, "That's sweet, but you would not have wanted to date me. I was a mess back then. I'm still a mess now."

"No, you're great! You were so sexy back then. Still are!" Pete replied.

"Maybe you've had enough wine for tonight," Jane said.

"Why?"

"Because you're making people uncomfortable."

"Am I? Are you uncomfortable, Hanna banana?"

"No, no I'm not. It's all good," I said.

"See Jane! It's all good!" Pete said as he poured another glass.

"Fine. I'm not going to argue with you when you're like this," Jane said.

We sat in silence again. Just listening to the crickets and watching the lightning bugs. I noticed how much more I could hear now that there wasn't the loud sound of the waves crashing on the shore.

"So, Jane…" Derrick said after a while. "Tell me about your lovely daughters."

"Well, Aubrey and Audrey are just the sweetest. They're four years old now, so they're really finding their personalities. Aubrey loves to do creative things, like draw and build things. She's a really good listener and never really acts out. Mostly keeps to herself. Audrey on the other hand can never sit still. She always wants to be on the move. Exploring and investigating. She wants to go outside all the time. And is never content with just sitting and relaxing."

"They sound lovely, and it seems like you've got your hands full," Derrick said.

"Oh yeah, they are a lot of work, but I love them."

"And are they mommy's girls, or daddy's girls?"

"Well, Nathan isn't really ever home. He's always supper busy with work. But they do love him. And he loves them. When he is home, they are all over him."

"That's good. And Pete, how's Elisa and Luke?" Derrick asked.

"Oh, they're great. Just great," he mumbled and slurred.

I knew Derrick didn't want to bring up Jack with me again, after seeing how uncomfortable it made me at dinner. So I stood up.

"Well, I think I'm going to take a walk to the beach and then go up to bed," I said.

"That sounds like a good idea. I'm beat," Derrick said as he stood up as well.

"I'm with you there. Come on, Pete, we're going to bed," Jane said as she tried to pull Pete out of his chair. Pete stood up and held on to Jane's arm. Jane turned off the fire and started walking with Pete draped around her. He wobbled and swayed as they crossed the grass.

"Goodnight!" Pete yelled.

"Goodnight, everyone," Jane said.

"Sleep well!" Derrick called back. Then he turned to me and said, "Good night, Hanna. Have a nice walk." And he headed across the yard toward the house. I went around back to the boardwalk, took my shoes off, and walked across the sand. I walked until I was ankle deep in the motionless water. I looked out on the sea. The sea, the darkest shade of black, looking like an endless abyss, like there's nothing even there. Just emptiness. And the night sky, only slightly lighter from the faint glows of the moon and stars. Above is black, and below is even blacker. The sky and the sea, the sea and the sky, two endless voids. There they sat, silent, and stretching on forever. After a while, I turned around, got my shoes, walked back to the house, and went to bed. As I lay there in the darkness, I realized just how quiet it is without the tides.

Day 2
Friday

Derrick

I woke up at the butt-crack of dawn. The light from the sun streamed in through the window and right onto my face. I rolled over and looked out the window which overlooked the front yard. The lawn was a vibrant green and the trees were waving gently in the wind. There was a slew of rabbits bouncing around the grounds, going this way and that. Stopping occasionally to munch on some grass. I looked up into the right corner of the ceiling and the spider was still there, in his web.

How crazy is it that anyone can look at a spider's web and not realize there is a god? Only a god could design something so beautiful, I thought.

I got up, got dressed, brushed my teeth, and headed downstairs. The old wooden planks creaked under my feet. Pete was making coffee in the kitchen, talking with Jane.

"Morning sleepyhead!" Pete called out to me when he heard me on the stairs.

I walked past the kitchen and said good morning to Pete and Jane, and I continued through the living room and out onto the front porch. Hanna was already there smoking a cigarette.

"Can I get one of those?" I asked.

"Sure. I didn't know priests smoked," Hanna said.

"Well, they do. And I'm not a priest. I just try to spread the good word wherever I go."

She slid a cigarette out of the tight, full pack, and handed it to me along with her lighter. I put it in my mouth, flicked the flame on, and dragged in. The morning breeze whipped the smoke from our cigarettes back and forth. I looked over at Hanna and realized she hadn't taken her eyes off something.

"What are you looking at?"

"That deer, the one that followed me here. He hasn't left," she said as she gestured out into the yard. I hadn't seen him when I first came out, but there he was, standing perfectly still. Just then, Pete and Jane came out onto the porch with four coffees. Pete handed me a cup and Jane handed one to Hanna.

"Has anyone seen or heard anything about the tides?" I asked.

"I haven't seen anything on my *Facebook* feed," Pete said.

"Same here, nothing on *Twitter* either," Jane added.

"Yeah, I can't find anything about it on *Google*," I said.

"Maybe it's not a big deal, like some natural phenomenon," Hanna said.

"Or maybe it's just happening here and no one else knows," Jane said.

"Or maybe it's not actually happening at all and we're all just hallucinating it," Pete said.

"That could be true," Jane said with a chuckle and added, "I haven't even looked out back to see if the water still isn't moving. Let's go."

The four of us, coffees in hand, walked down off the front porch and went around the side of the house. Almost immediately, even from a distance, we could tell the waves weren't moving. But we kept walking toward the ocean to get a closer look, as if we didn't want to believe it.

The water was still undulating, bobbing up and down, but there was no tide. No waves coming up the beach and sliding back down across the sand. Hanna took her sandals off and walked into the water up to her knees.

"It's really warm," she said.

"Warm?" Pete asked.

"Yeah, way warmer than yesterday. It was freezing yesterday and now it's like a heated pool. I wonder if that has anything to do with the tide stopping," she said.

"Of course it does. It means the world is ending," Pete chuckled.

"No, it doesn't," I said.

"Yeah, don't say things like that," Jane added.

Hanna walked out of the water and slipped her sandals back on. And as we turned to walk back to the house, it all of a sudden got really quiet. Extremely quiet. We all looked at each other in confusion.

"Why is it so quiet?" Jane asked.

"The wind, it's stopped," Hanna said.

"She's right; there's no wind," Pete said.

It was true; the normal jet engine-like whipping of wind that was constant when standing on the beach... had stopped. There was absolutely no movement in the air. Not a single gust. Not a single sound. Compared to a second before, the silence was quite literally deafening.

"Okay, this is fucked up. What is going on here?" Jane said.

Hanna pulled out a cigarette and lit it as she handed me one. She held out her cigarette in front of here to show how the smoke coming from the tip just rose up slowly. Straight up. Not a hint of movement in any direction. It curled slowly in the air, higher and higher.

"Strange. Not even a slight breeze," I said as I mimicked her and held out my cigarette.

"The smoke is acting like it does when you smoke inside," Pete said.

"And you would know that how? Do much smoking?" Jane asked.

"Not now Jane, this is serious. Now Mr. Holy Man, what do you make if this? Is the end nigh?" Pete said.

"Of course not. Again, it's probably some ecological phenomenon or something. The wind and the tides will come back. It's nothing. This is not god's work," I said.

But it just might be, I thought.

We all started walking again, up back toward the house. When we got to the front door Hanna asked if we could help push her car from down the road up to the driveway, a task none of us wanted to do.

"I can't push it myself," Hanna pleaded.

"Okay, let's go and get this over with," I said.

We started walking down the driveway and a few seconds later, we heard a clip-clop sound coming from behind us. Everyone looked back except Hanna.

"Don't mind him," she said, still looking forward. "He goes where I go."

"That damn deer. Why does he like you so much?" I asked.

"I don't know. I don't know if he even does like me at all. Maybe he hates me. Maybe he's waiting for the right time to trample me or stab me with his antlers."

"I wonder what he wants," I said.

"If you could get got to talk to him and ask, that'd be great," Hanna remarked.

"That's not how it works. Sorry."

"That's too bad," she said sarcastically.

We walked the rest of the way in silence, extra silence. The wind was still nowhere to be heard. The trees on either side of the road stood there like statues of stone. Not a rustle, not a sway. Only the clip-clop sound of hooves behind us. Finally, we got to Hanna's car. She opened the door and got in the driver seat. The three of us went around back. Hanna put it in neutral and we started to push.

Hanna steered, we pushed. It was slow at first but luckily there was a slight downhill slope in the road leading to the house. Eventually, we only needed to give a slight nudge every once in a while, and Hanna had enough speed for a few feet. And of course, the deer walked alongside the car, next to Hanna. To keep us occupied, Hanna told us the whole story about how the deer caused her to crash her car. And all I kept thinking was:

Now that's an act of god.

We got back to the driveway and Hanna put the car in park. Pete, Jane, and I went into the house and sat in the living room. Hanna stayed outside and set up an appointment with a tow truck to come get her on Monday. By the time she came in and joined us, we were on the topic of god again.

"So you really don't think the tides stopping and the wind stopping is a sign of the apocalypse?" Pete asked me.

"Oh, come on, you don't really believe in that shit do you?" Hanna interjected.

"I don't know. Maybe," Pete answered.

"Religion was invented for this very reason, to provide answers to an unfathomable world. But was very quickly and purposely altered into a tool intended to control. Control by taking advantage of people who are afraid. It convinces people to do good so they can be rewarded, instead of doing good just for the sake of it. And furthermore, the definition of what 'good' is, is distilled and filtered through the arbitrary conceptions of that religion. The parameters of which are built into the foundation of the religion with the deliberate intention to force people to live a certain way. And they enforce these 'holy laws' by suggesting any who break these laws will be punished. It's basic fear-based control."

"What's wrong with fear-based control? That's why we have laws. If you rob a bank, you will go to jail. Thus, the fear of jail stops people from robbing a bank," I said.

"That's a different structure though. That's using fear of punishment to *stop* you from doing certain things. Religion uses fear of punishment to force you to *do* certain things. If you don't do x, y, and z, then you will be punished. For example, I was raised Catholic, and I was told I had to pray every night before bed. And when I was little, one night I fell asleep before I said my prayers, and I woke up in the middle of the night with the overwhelming feeling of dread and fear because I forgot to say my prayers. I got on the floor and prayed, but I couldn't fall back asleep because I was sure I was going to hell. No belief system should instill that kind of fear into children."

"Well, that just sounds like you were misunderstanding the teachings, or you were just taught incorrectly. Whoever taught you should have made sure you understood that you wouldn't go to hell just because you forgot your prayers."

"That may be the case, but that's beside the point. The point is that the very existence of religion allowed for someone to instill that fear in me. If that religion never existed, I never would have been afraid to fall asleep without saying my prayers."

"So, you really don't believe in anything?"

"Not in religion. It's the scourge of our time."

"Now come on, it's not that bad," Jane said.

"Oh, yes it is. First off, it's inherently bigoted. It teaches an 'us versus them' mentality. We're right, they're wrong. Furthermore, it has people live their lives based off delusions. Belief in religion is and should be considered a mental disorder. It's a form of insanity. There's a reason no one believes Poseidon stopped those waves out there. It's because that would be insane to say that. Any modern religion is the same thing. I cannot understand why it's so normal and fine for people to believe in ancient mythology still. You say Poseidon stopped the waves. We would laugh at you. But say it was god, and we all take you seriously."

By the time Hanna finished her rant, Pete and Jane had gotten up and went into the kitchen. It was just he and me left in the living room. We talked a little while longer and I could see that there was no changing her mind, and obviously she wasn't going to change mine. When we finally agreed to disagree, it was early evening. Where Jane and Pete were the whole time, I had no idea.

All the windows were open in the house but not a curtain was swaying. The sun was setting over the calm and silent sea. Hanna and I walked into the kitchen to start making dinner, and just then, Pete and Jane came down the stairs.

"Where were you guys?" I asked.

"We were both tired, so we took naps," Pete said.

"You ready for dinner?" Hanna said.

"I'm starving."

Hanna and I finished making dinner—burgers, a veggie one for Hanna. We took the food out on the back porch to watch the sunset. We ate in mostly silence. I picked at the peeling paint on the wooden arm of my chair. If I was being honest to the others, I'd tell them that the unmoving tides and lack of wind were concerning me.

In the silence, Hanna spoke up and said, "I had a strange dream last night."

"Oh yeah? What about?" Pete asked.

"Well, I'm standing in the middle of a clearing in the woods. Naked. It's the middle of the night, but there's so much light because the moon is so full and unnaturally big and bright. All around me are deep green ferns and ground cover. And standing in front of me is that deer. He walks up to me and licks my face like a dog. He nuzzles his nose in my chest. Then he takes a step back and rams his antlers into my stomach. He pulls them up and out, ripping open my stomach. All of my organs start falling out, and I drop to my knees trying to grab my organs and stuff them back into my body. I look up and the deer is gone. Then I wake up. What do you make of that?"

"I think it means you're scared shitless of that deer," Pete said.

"Nah, I'm actually pretty calm when I'm around him."

"I think it symbolizes you trying to put yourself or your life back together," Jane said.

"Maybe. I do feel kind of all over the place right now. I feel like I'm in pieces."

"Or it could mean you're supposed to spill your guts and not hold anything in."

We didn't talk much for the rest of dinner. After we finished eating, Jane cleaned up and did the dishes. Pete went to go start the fire and get the wine, of course. I decided to take a walk down the beach alone to watch the sunset. The air was warm and unmoving. It reminded me of the day I started to believe in god.

It was a warm summer evening, and I was at a beach walking alone, far from any people. The sun was touching the water's horizon, ready to disappear. As I was walking along the shore, the sun glimmered in the water in such a way that it caught my eye. But when the light glare off the water faded, I saw someone about 20 yards out. It was a small boy.

At first, I thought he was playing but soon realized he was flailing around. He was drowning. I ran into the water, swam out, grabbed the boy, and pulled him back to shore. He was alright. Turned out he lived up on the hill and snuck out to go for a swim and swam too far out. I brought him home to his worried parents. And I realized that god must have put me at that exact place at that exact time, and made the sun's glint in the water catch my attention, all so I could save that boy's life.

I was not religious before then. And I've been steadfast in my new beliefs ever since then. But I do sometimes wonder if I'm just using religion to explain a very impactful and substantial moment. Searching for an explanation. Maybe Hanna was right. And if there is a god, why would he let that little boy almost drown in the first place. We explain that away by saying it's all part of god's plan. And he works in mysterious ways. But if you stop to think about that, like really think about it, you quickly realize how ridiculous that is. I decide to head back and rejoin the others around the fire. I walked back along the silent, tideless, and windless shore as the sun's last rays dropped below the water. When I got back to the fire, the three of them were just standing there, staring up at the sky.

"Does that look like another full moon?" Pete asked.

I looked up. "Yeah, it does. It looks the exact same as yesterday," I said.

"Yeah, but, the day before and the day after a full moon, it's always hard to tell," Jane said.

"Sure, but it was a full moon the night before we got here. And then last night it wasn't any different, and tonight is the same. In fact, the moon looks a bit brighter," Pete said.

"It's nothing," I said.

"Yeah, listen to the priest," Hanna said, giving me a wink and handing me a cigarette.

We all sat down around the fire, which unlike the night before, was flickering straight up. The flames and the smoke weren't being blown every which way. A little blessing, I guess, no smoke blowing in our faces. The night wore on and Pete and Hanna were getting drunk.

"So, you really don't believe in anything, any higher power, or god?" Pete asked Hanna.

"No, I don't. Because I'm not insane."

"Why is it insane to believe?" Jane asked.

"Religion should be considered a mental disorder. Think about it. If I told you that I genuinely believed in leprechauns and that they brought me gold every night. And on the weekends, I went into the woods and rode unicorns. You would think I was crazy, delusional, hallucinatory, and should be on medication. So, why is that any different than believing in any religion? Why is that normal? Because it's been around a long time? That's not a good enough reason. But still, we give it a free pass. Even though there is no more proof of gods, angels, demons, and ghosts than there is proof of leprechauns and unicorns. Why do none of us believe the oceans are controlled by Poseidon, and lighting is from Zeus? Because that would be insanity if we believed that. Believing in religion is a form of insanity," Hanna said.

"I would not think you were insane if you believed in leprechauns and unicorns. I'd think you were eccentric, whimsical, may be a bit odd. But not insane," Pete said.

"Well, then you're the only person on Earth who would think that. And I really don't believe you. If I lived my life by the belief in leprechauns, truly, seriously framed my existence around that belief, you would not think I was a bit odd. You would be worried about me and my ability to function in the world."

"But we need to believe in something!" Pete exclaimed.

"No, no we don't. It's really easy," Hanna said.

"Well, I'm freaking out about the tides, and the wind, and the moon. And I need some sort of explanation. So, fuck it. Let's drink if it's the end of the world."

"I think you've had enough," Jane said.

"You don't tell me when I've had enough!" Pete yelled, as he smashed his wine glass against the stone fire pit. A piece of glass flew and hit Jane in the cheek, cutting her pretty badly.

"What the fuck man!" I said.

"Oh my god! I'm so sorry. I did not mean to do that." Pete said. He reached out to Jane, but she pushed him away as she got up holding her cheek and walking toward the house.

"Maybe you have had enough," Hanna said.

"Maybe I have. I should go in and make sure she's okay."

Pete got up and went into the house. Hanna and I sat in the breezeless night, taking in the quiet.

After a while, Hanna said, "So, you really don't think all this stuff is god's doing?"

"I honestly don't know," I said. Then I got up, said goodnight, and went in to go to bed. I don't know how long Hanna sat alone in the silence.

Day 3
Saturday

Jane

I woke up and felt my cheek, still sore. I rolled over and faced Pete.

How did it end up like this? I wonder why it had to be this way. Can you love two people at the same time? Especially when one of them is so flawed? I have to end it. Today. For the sake of my husband and kids.

Pete stirred and slowly woke up.

"You better get back your bed before everyone else wakes up."

"Yeah, you're right. How's your cheek?"

"It's fine, not too big of a deal. But what is a big deal is your drinking."

"I know. I'll stop drinking… for you though."

We kissed and Pete got up and snuck back to his room. Moments later, Hanna got up for her morning cigarette. I could hear her walk down the stairs, across the living room, and out the door on to the front porch.

"That damn deer is finally gone!" Hanna yelled from the front porch. I lay in bed for a few more minutes thinking about the situation I was in. I was falling down both sides of the blades here. I loved my husband and children, but I loved Pete too. Each of them made me feel good. Each of them appealed to different sides of my personality.

I got up, got dressed, and took the bandage off my cheek. The cut seemed to be healing fine. I brushed my teeth and headed downstairs. Derrick had breakfast already started. I poured a cup of coffee and went out back to call my husband to check in.

"Hello."

"Hey there, sweetie," he said.

"How are the kids doing?" I asked.

"Pretty good. Aubrey wants to talk to you."

"Okay, put her on."

"Mommy?"

"Hi darling, is there something the matter?"

"Yeah, I have these little black dots in my eyes. I see them when my eyes are closed and even when they're open. They move around too. Are they aliens?"

"No sweetheart, they're not aliens. Everyone has those; they're called floaters. They're just little specks of dirt and dust that are on your eyeball. So you don't have anything to worry about. But why didn't Daddy tell you that?"

"I didn't want to talk to him about it. I wanted to talk to you."

"Well, that's sweet, darling. But you don't have to worry."

"Okay, thank you, Mommy. Here's Daddy."

"Floaters, huh? That's what she was worried about?" he said.

"Guess so."

"How are things going there?"

"Well, remember when I told you that the tides stopped moving?"

"Yeah?"

"So, yesterday, the wind stopped. There's literally no wind."

"Okay, now I'm getting worried. That sounds like some sort of storm or hurricane is coming. You need to get out of there."

"We're fine. We've looked it up and there's nothing on the internet about it. Plus, we're leaving in a few days anyways."

"Alright, I'll see you soon, sweetie."

"See you soon."

I walked out to join Hanna on the porch. She was looking out in the yard for the deer.

"He's finally gone," she said. "I actually kind of miss him."

"Man, without the tides and winds, it is really quiet."

"Yeah, but it feels even quieter today. I can't put my finger on it."

Just then, Derrick came out to have a cigarette with Hanna, so I knew I had some time to talk to Pete. I popped back inside to find Pete in the kitchen.

"Are they out there?" Pete asked as he leaned in to kiss me. I pulled away.

"Listen. We need to talk. I can't keep doing this. I can't keep loving two people at the same time. It hurts too much."

"You're ending it? After I said I would leave my wife for you?"

"That's one of the reasons I want to end it. I don't want you to break up your family."

"But it could be worth it. We could have a great life together."

"We could, and I'm sure we would. But we already have great lives."

"Am I not enough?"

"You are plenty enough, flaws and all. You appeal to sides of me that make me feel alive. You bring me such joy and so much satisfaction."

He just turned and stared out the back window. And I thought about love and its messiness—how you can be attracted to more than one person at a time and how we desire love so much that just having one person isn't enough.

I thought about why we want to be in love… why we desire it so strongly. It's because you get to show someone else the very best parts of yourself. The parts of you that you think are just amazing. The parts you want other people to see. You get to share that with them, and that is the part of love that makes us feel good. It's like when we were kids and we got all excited for show and tell. Because we got to bring in what we thought was our coolest toy and share it with our friends.

Heads filled with thoughts of, *Who wouldn't want to see and hear about this toy?*

Same thing with love. There are parts of us that we want other people to see so badly because we think they're so cool, or desirable, or attractive. I'm sure we all have been out on our own and did something nice or said something cool and thought:

Man! I wish someone was here to see that.

Of course there's the biological reasons we love and why love feels good. Evolution makes us feel love so that we can mate and procreate. But I really think—psychologically-speaking—why it feels so good is because we get to be the person we want to be. We get to be our best selves. And we get to see the best selves of other people.

"Okay," Pete said after some time.

"Really?"

"Yes, it makes the most sense."

"It was nice while it lasted. And we'll always be friends."

We walked together back into the living room where Hanna and Derrick were talking about religion again.

"Hey, I have a question for you, guys. I'm actually writing a book with characters like you, all three of you as a matter of fact, and would love to interview you three about your different religious beliefs. You represent three distinct points on the spectrum. The firm believer in Derrick..." who smiled nervously, "the undecided in Pete, and the nonbeliever in Hanna."

"Let's do it!" Hanna said.

"Yeah? You're in? What about you two?"

"Sure, why not?" Pete said.

"I guess that'd be okay," Derrick said.

"Okay, do you mind if I record this?" I asked as I pulled out my phone. No one objected.

"Let's start with the believer, Derrick. What are your thoughts on religion?"

"Can we maybe start with someone else?"

"Sure, let's start with Pete. What are your thoughts on religion?"

"Well, I'm not too sure. I definitely think that there's something bigger going on. But who knows? My tiny monkey brain can't wrap itself around those types of ideas. Maybe this is just a computer program. Or maybe we were put here by aliens. You know?"

"Do you really believe that there are aliens out there?" Derrick asked.

"Of course, I do. It's literally more illogical to think that we are the only ones than it is to think there are other sentient beings out there."

"Whatever, you're nuts."

"If we've only been around for about 40 to 70 thousand years, and we've only had solid science for a few hundred years, imagine a planet with a life form on it that began to evolve into advanced sentient beings, but they started 100,000 years ago, or half a million, or a million, or hell, a billion years ago. Think about how much time there has been for life to evolve. If we humans have not only naturally occurred on this planet but also evolved relatively quickly on the cosmic scale, then it can only be deduced that it has happened out there many times over, and on many different planets."

"But then why haven't we had any concrete evidence that they exist? The Fermi Paradox, right? If they're out there, and they're so advanced, as would seem to be likely, then why have we not seen any evidence of their footprints in the cosmos?"

"Because the Fermi Paradox is predicated on the belief that if there is life out there, it is similar to us, and that they have, or at one point had, similar evolution and technology. A lot of scientists think that life can only emerge in a few very limited and specific ways, with stringent requirements. But again, that is so illogical. Life will arise and evolve in any way it can. Just because we evolved this way, on this planet, doesn't mean that it can only ever be this way. And all the planets out there are so different that we should conclude that the life on those planets are utterly and completely inconceivable to us. And because they are so vastly different from us, then their technology would be as vastly different as well. Which means, their existence, their presence would not be detectable by our technology. No matter how advanced they get, and advanced we get, our science and technology are totally incompatible. It would be like expecting the bacteria living at the deepest depths of the ocean to be able to detect our human technology and presence. They can't and never will. We will come and go, without them ever knowing. And it's the same situation when it comes to the cosmos. We can never know what life on other planets is like, unless we see it firsthand. And we won't. The only way we will ever find other life out there, is if by the very slim chance that they did evolve similarly to us, and somehow our two planet's technologies can detect each other. But that doesn't seem statistically likely. There are too many variables. So, we probably won't ever know the truth. But I do believe there are perhaps billions of planets out there with sentient life on them, at different phases of evolution. Whole civilizations have sprouted, evolved, peaked, and disappeared all without us ever knowing, and we never will because their footprint, their residue, their presence is undetectable to us. Just like our presence is undetectable to them," Pete said.

"Well, shit. Way to give me an existential crisis," Hanna laughed.

"Hanna, what are your thoughts?"

"Well, I think religion sprouted in our brains as a way to explain what we at the time couldn't explain. The first humans had no idea that when the sun went down, that it would for sure come back up. They were scared. And when it did come back up, they invented stories about the sun, the moon, the rain, lightning, and other things that they could not comprehend. I also think that the first humans to have an inner monologue thought that some other being was talking to them, telling them things. They had no idea it was just their own mind. So, those people made claims that gods—let's call them gods—were talking to them. It was a perfect storm of lack of understanding and the emerging of imagination. All religion comes from people, normal, everyday, plain old people. It was invented accidentally. Used to explain things. And then turned into a tool for control."

"Interesting. Derrick, do you have a rebuttal?"

"I think she's right."

"Excuse me? Did I just hear you correctly?" Hanna said.

"Yeah, I think you're right. Or maybe. I don't know."

"Well, this is a surprise," I said.

"I'm having a crisis of faith here, okay."

"Why's that?" I asked.

"It's all this stuff happening. The tides, the wind, the full moons. My kneejerk response is to say it's god. But maybe I'm just being like those early humans and using god as a filler for something I don't understand. Maybe the whole of religion is just one big made-up story. Maybe there are aliens. Hell! There probably are. It makes sense. Maybe religion was an accident, like Hanna said. Maybe I don't believe anymore. I didn't used to believe until I had a traumatic experience saving a drowning boy's life. And maybe that trauma caused me to want to believe. Out of fear. Out of not knowing. Out of not being able to explain something. All I know is that I need to take a walk. I'll be back."

Derrick got up and walked out the back door toward the beach. It didn't feel right continuing on after his revelation. I couldn't believe he was going through that type of crisis.

"Well, I guess that's the end of that," I said.

"I'll make dinner," Pete said.

"I think I'll go have a cigarette," Hanna said.

I followed Pete into the kitchen. I was going to tell him it's over. He was getting the pans out to make burgers.

"Pete, we need to talk about something," I said.

"What's that? You want to sneak away for a quickie?"

"No. I need to tell you something. It's going to be hard to hear, but it's over."

"What's over?"

"Us."

"Us?"

"Yes… us. We need to stop seeing each other."

"So, that's it. You've had your fun and now you don't want anything to do with me?"

"That's not it at all. This is very hard for me."

"Do you love me?"

"Of course, I do."

"Then leave your husband."

"I can't do that. Unlike you and your wife, I actually love my husband."

"I love my wife!"

"Come on. Be honest. You don't really love her."

"Okay, you're right. I hate my life. I would leave her for you. Let's do it."

"Let's destroy our lives for something that might not even be good?"

"Yes."

"No. We aren't doing that. At least I'm not. You can leave your wife if you want. Maybe you should if you hate your life so much. But I love my life, and this thing with us is only complicating it."

Just then, Hanna came into the kitchen.

"Burgers again?"

"Yeah. And Jane has volunteered to take over. Haven't you, Jane?"

"Sure."

Pete walked out the back door without saying another word.

"Did I interrupt something?" Hanna asked.

"Sort of. Look, I don't want you to freak out but…"

"You and Pete are sleeping together."

"How'd you know?"

"You two aren't exactly James Bond when it comes to hiding things. It's pretty obvious."

"You can't tell Derrick. He'll get all high and mighty about adultery being wrong."

"Maybe not now, after his little religious meltdown. He probably won't care. In fact, he probably already knows. So,

I take it by Pete's attitude that you decided to end it and he didn't want to? He stormed out of here pretty quickly."

"Yeah, he wanted me to leave my husband and he would leave is wife. I told him that's not happening. And that we can't see each other anymore."

"I'm sorry to hear that. It must have been hard. Let me help you make dinner."

Hanna and I made dinner, and eventually the boys came back. We sat outside eating. We all had our reasons to be silent. Derrick was embarrassed. Pete was mad. I was sad. And Hanna felt awkward. But towards the end of dinner, Derrick spoke up.

"I had a pretty freaky dream last night."

"Tell us about it."

"Well, Hanna, you remember that spider in my room?"

"Yeah."

"So, there's been this spider up in the corner of my room since we got here. And in my dream, I wake up at dawn and the spider is up in the corner, except he's giant. He takes up half the room. And in a deep, otherworldly voice, he says to me, 'You're drowning… You're drowning… You're drowning.' Over and over and over again. And each time he says it, it gets harder to breathe. And right before I pass out from lack of air, I wake up. And guess what? The spider was gone from the corner of my room."

"That is pretty weird," Hanna said.

"That's one of the many reasons I'm having second thoughts about my religion. I feel like that dream is trying to tell me something."

"But what?" I asked.

"I have no idea. It's obviously linked to the drowning boy I saved. Am I the boy? Am I god for saving him? Is life all just random chance? I don't know."

"Maybe the spider is god and he's telling you that you're drowning in confusion about your faith."

"That could be it."

We finished dinner and headed over to the fire pit. Pete grabbed the wine and already started drinking before the fire was even lit. We all talked for a while about things and then there was a silence. Pete blurted out, "Jane and I are sleeping together!"

"We know," Hanna and Derrick said at the same time. "We don't care."

Silence fell around us again. And that's when I noticed something. Or rather didn't notice something. There was something different about tonight. It took me quite a while sitting in the silence to pinpoint it. When I finally did figure it out, I spoke up.

"Does anyone notice anything different or strange about tonight?"

"You mean other than the fact that it's yet another night with a completely full moon? And there's still no tides or wind?" Hanna said.

"Other than that. Think carefully. Take note of your surroundings. It's hard to notice at first because it's so normal and constant that it goes unnoticed most of the time. We tune it out. But once you realize what it is, you can't stop noticing it," I replied.

Everyone sat for a moment, confused, with scowls and furrowed brows plastered on their faces. And then I saw it start clicking for them, and their perplexed expressions transitioned to ones of shock and disbelief. Pete was the first to say something.

"My god… there aren't any bugs."

"Precisely," I said. "No bugs anywhere. No buzzing of mosquitoes, no chirping of crickets, no glows of lighting bugs."

"The bugs are gone? Just gone?" Derrick said.

"I think it's all animals. I noticed earlier that there weren't any seagulls. And my deer is gone too," Hanna said.

"Now that you mention it, like I told you guys earlier, there has been a spider in its web up in the corner of my room ever since we got here on Thursday. When I got up this morning, it wasn't there, but I didn't think anything of it at the time," Derrick said.

"What in the hell is going on? First the tides stopped. The wind stopped. Now all the bugs and animals are gone. Then there's been a full moon every night. Maybe it really is the end of days," Pete said as he looked up at the full moon.

"Shut up!" Derrick said.

"I'm actually starting to get worried. I want to leave tomorrow instead of Monday," I said. "First thing in the morning, I'm packing and going home."

"I think that might be a good idea," Pete said.

"Yeah, I'm with you guys on this one," Derrick said.

"Oh, come on. It's nothing. And if it is something, we've got such a beautiful spot to watch it all end."

"That's easy for you to say. You don't have a life!" Pete said.

"Pete!" I said.

"Fuck off, Pete," Hanna said.

"Let's all just calm down and go to bed. We'll leave in the morning," I said.

Day 4
Sunday

Pete

I woke up with a splitting headache. The room was spinning, and I could hear Jane shouting from downstairs.

"Come on! Let's go!"

I pulled myself up and found that all my stuff was already packed.

Did I do that, or did Jane?

I wearily grabbed my things and headed downstairs. Hanna, Derrick, and Jane were waiting in the living room. I pulled out my phone to see what time it was, but the screen was black. The battery must have died in the night.

"What time is it?" I asked.

"I don't know, but I'm about to call an *Uber* to get us out of here."

She pulled her phone out and looked at it, confused.

"My phone's not turning on."

Derrick and Hanna checked their phones too, and they found the same thing to be happening with theirs as well. We all pulled out our chargers and plugged our phones in. Waited a few minutes and still nothing.

"Why aren't our phones working now?" Jane asked.

"I have no clue," Derrick said.

"What do you think we should do?" I asked.

"I know what I'm doing," Jane said. "I'm walking."

"You're just going to walk?"

"Yep, I'm just going to start walking. Even though last night I had a dream that I started walking down the road and it just kept going on forever. And eventually, night fell, and I got lost in the woods somehow."

"Well, then maybe you shouldn't walk then," I said.

"I'm doing it. Maybe at some point I'll be able to get cell service."

"Well, then I guess I'm going to sit on the beach drinking, waiting for the world to end."

"Derrick and Hanna, look after him, okay?"

"We will."

And with that, Jane headed down the driveway onto the road leading out of here. I grabbed a bottle of whisky and went to the back to sit on the beach. Derrick and Hanna sat with me.

"So, Derrick, are you still unsure if this is god or not?"

"Honestly, I don't know. It doesn't match anything in the Bible. I see no correlation whatsoever between the four things."

"I do," Hanna said. "Water, the tides stopped. Air, the wind stopped. Earth, the animals and bugs went away. And now fire, our technology; it's our modern fire. Don't you see? It's the four elements."

"Yeah, I guess you could be right. It does make some sort of sense. But why is the question? And for that I have to believe in something."

"But what makes you think that your religion is the right one? I mean the gall and boldness of you to think that your religion is more valid than any other. Do you not realize that if everything about your life was the exact same except instead of Christianity you were taught Buddhism, you would be saying with the same surety that Buddhism is the right religion? Which proves that it all comes down to culture and conditioning. No religion is more valid than any other. They're all equally as insane. You can't use an old book as proof of anything. Imagine someone 500 years from now saying, 'We must follow the word of our lord and savior Harry Potter.' You would call them insane."

After there was a lull in their banter and I was good and drunk, I blurted out, "I lost my license for drunk driving, and I drink because I hate my life. I want to leave my wife and be with Jane, but Jane doesn't want that. She doesn't ever want to see me again. What does god have to say about that?"

"God has nothing to say about that. That's your problem to fix. If Jane doesn't want to be with you, then that option is out of the question. So, you could either leave your wife and go thought that whole mess or stick it out and see what happens."

I had finished the bottle by the time he was done talking and was starting to pass out. The last thing I remember was my head hitting the sand.

While I was out, I had a dream that I was a little boy running around the house playing. My dad was drunk in the living room and I ran past him and knocked over his glass of scotch. He got so mad that he beat me until I was unrecognizable. And then he picked me up and squeezed my like a lime into a glass and drank me.

The next thing I remember was it being dark outside and I was on the couch in the living room. Jane was standing over me slapping me in the face.

"Wake up, you moron. Dinner's ready."

"So I take it you didn't find any cell service or make it to the end of the road?"

"No, I turned around when it started getting dark. It looks like we're stuck here for the night."

"I say, in the morning, we all walk together, safer that way," Derrick said.

"Sounds like a plan," Hanna replied.

We ate dinner, this time not in silence. Jane and I were arguing over our relationship. And Hanna and Derrick over religion.

After dinner, we sat by the fire. I decided not to drink. It was actually so peaceful. No sound from the tides, no blowing wind, no bugs chirping, no phones to look at. Just us and another full moon.

Day 5
Monday

Hanna

We all woke up to the sound of our phones buzzing and ringing from texts and missed calls.

Well, our phones work now, I thought. *That's good at least.*

"Our phones are working again!" Jane shouted.

"Let's try to call an *Uber* to get us the fuck out of here," Pete said.

"The spider is back in the corner of my room," Derrick called out.

I quickly ran over to the window to see if my deer was back. He was. There were squirrels and rabbits running through the yard, and there in the middle of it all was my deer. He came back for me.

We gathered up our luggage and went downstairs. The silence was gone. We went out onto the back deck and there were the tides, flowing in and out, up and down the shoreline. The wind was strong, and the gulls were loud in the sky, gliding on the breeze. The leaves rustled in the wind, and all was back to normal.

Pete and Jane were the first to call *Ubers*. Separate ones this time. Then Derrick called a cab to get back to the airport. And I called a tow truck to come and get me and my wreck of a car. The four of us took a walk down to the beach and sat in the sand for a while. None of us said anything. One by one, as our rides arrived, we got up. Pete's *Uber* came first. We said our goodbyes, and he walked back into the house, got his things and left. Jane's *Uber* came next, we said our goodbyes, and she was gone. Derrick's cab came, we hugged and he told me he had some thinking to do, and we should keep in touch.

A few hours passed with me just sitting on the beach. The other three had gone. It was just me, waiting for the tow truck. Just me, the ocean, and the deer. The damn dear was still just standing there, out in the front yard. I decided to walk over to him, just to see if he'd let me pet him. I quietly walked up to him, pausing for a moment between each step. He never moved. Eventually, I was standing face to face with him. I lifted my hand and moved it forward slowly. The deer didn't move, just stared at me, right in my eyes. I inched my hand closer to its head. Still, he stayed standing calmly but stiffly. Finally, I touched the front of his face with the tips of my fingers and slid them up along the coarse fur. I put them back down and stroked his face again. And then a third time, and a fourth. Then he seemed to relax the tension in his body. He took a slight step backward, blinked, and lowered his head while still maintaining eye contact. I stepped back, unsure of what he was going to do. But all he did was calmly turn around and walk toward the woods.

When he reached the tree line, he stopped and looked back at me with what felt like fondness. And then, with one quick jump, he entered the forest, disappearing among the green and brown of the trees. For a moment, I could hear the leaves and sticks rustling and cracking as he ran through the woods. And then he was gone.

I figured I should walk to the end of the driveway to wait at my car for the tow truck. But first, I walked to the back deck and took a long look at the sea. The tides moving in and out. The wind blowing. The gulls were screeching. The sun high in the clear blue sky. Just like the paintings in the house.

Maybe I'll get back to the shore again soon. Who knows? Maybe I'll move to the shore. Fuck it, I thought. *Why not?*

www.ingramcontent.com/pod-product-compliance
Lightning Source LLC
Chambersburg PA
CBHW061629130726

47996CB00003B/1188